For my Grandchildren Libbs, Madison, William,
Lily-Mae, Freddie, Alfie and Bradley.

To my wife Alison and granddaughter Libby for their
comments and suggestions which are greatly appreciated.
Also for their positive support that has enabled me to do this.

DOGCHESTER PD

The Great Bone Robbery

First published in Great Britain in 2021 by:
MAGIC MOUSE BOOKS
An imprint of PARTNERSHIP PUBLISHING

Magic Mouse

Text Copyright © Sam Shepherd
Illustration Copyright © Sarah-Leigh Wills

A CIP catalogue record for this book is available from the British Library.
Paperback ISBN 978-1-7399246-7-6

Illustration and Design by: Happydesigner

Book Published by:
PARTNERSHIP PUBLISHING Lincolnshire, United Kingdom
www.partnershippublishing.co.uk

Printed in England.
Partnership Publishing is committed to a sustainable future for our business, our readers and
our planet. This book is made from paper certified by the Forestry Stewardship Council (FSC),
an organisation dedicated to promoting responsible management of forest resources.

DOGCHESTER PD

The Great Bone Robbery

Written by
Sam Shepherd

Illustrated by Sarah-Leigh Wills

In the middle of Boneland lies the city of Dogchester.
Its pride and joy is the police department, Dogchester PD.

These are stories about the adventures of the brave
dogs who keep the people of Dogchester safe.

It was another warm sunny day and Chief Growler looked out from his office window and saw his beautiful city shimmering in the sunlight.

The chief was from a long line of police chiefs within his family whose pictures proudly hung in his office.

Suddenly, the door to his office burst open and in ran Deputy Chief Gruff. "There's been a robbery at The Boneland Bank!" she shouted.

"How much has been taken?" asked Chief Growler. "1500 golden bones have been taken from the main vault," replied Gruff.

Chief Growler stroked his chin. "That's a big job.
Get a patrol there as quickly as you can, and tell
Detectives Snooper and Snatcher to get down there
and see what clues they can find."

Deputy Gruff left the office and went to the radio room.
She spoke to the officer who was taking down details
from the bank manager on the telephone.

"Officer Noodles, please send Detectives Snooper
and Snatcher with a car straight to the bank."

The poodle replied, "I'm Officer Doodles Ma'am;
Noodles is on a coffee break." Gruff made a mental note
to self to ask whose idea it had been to hire identical twins.

Down at the bank Detective Inspector Snatcher and his assistant Sergeant (Sgt) Snooper were looking for clues.

Suddenly, WHOOSH! Snooper disappeared.

There then came a loud BUMP! And a muffled "OW!" from a large hole that had been hidden behind some crates in the vault.

Snatcher investigated the hole with his torch and saw Sgt Snooper in a crumpled heap below. He was covered in dust. "I think this is where they got in boss," said Snooper painfully.

"Really?" said Snatcher. "Your powers of deduction never cease to amaze me. Snooper." Even though he joked about him, Snooper was the best detective he had worked with.

Snatcher then climbed into the hole and
he suddenly found himself stuck.

"Snooper, give me a pull to help me through the hole,"
he said. Snooper got hold of both legs and pulled.

He pulled again and on the third pull Snatcher
came crashing through.

"OOff!!" shouted Snooper as his boss landed
firmly on top of him.

Snatcher lifted himself off his unfortunate Sergeant
who was pressed flat against the floor.

"Don't just lie there Snooper!" he shouted,
"Get up and let's see where this tunnel leads!!"

Snooper got up in a daze. 'The boss really needs to cut down on the treats,' he thought to himself. He turned on his torch and the two detectives headed off down the long dark tunnel.

As they went further into the tunnel, Snooper's nose started twitching. "What is it?" asked Snatcher.

"Chilli and tacos," said Snooper.
Snatcher rubbed his chin and said, "That can only mean one thing! The Chihuahua boys!"

The Chihuahua boys were a very naughty group of dogs who frequently took things that did not belong to them, but they were not easy to catch.

At the other end of the tunnel, the opening led into a large room where the Chihuahua boys were sitting eating chilli and tacos and counting the large number of golden bones that were in a pile in front of them.

"Well boys," said the gang boss. "We have hit the jackpot this time. We had better get rid of them quickly."

"Do you think the cops will catch up with us Boss?"
said one of the gang.
"They couldn't catch a cold, never mind us,"
the boss replied.

Little did he know that underneath them Snooper and Snatcher were gaining fast. Back in the tunnel the two detectives were underneath the hole that led to where the Chihuahua boys were hiding.

The gang had left a set of ladders leading up into the hole,
having forgotten to take them away when they had climbed up.
Snatcher started slowly climbing up the ladder.
When he got to the top he started to climb through.

Again he got stuck and hissed at Snooper. "Give us a push then come through behind me." Snooper started pushing and shoving and suddenly POP!! Snatcher shot into the room like a cork out of a bottle.

He landed right in the middle of the gang,
completely startling them.
"Cops!" shouted the boss, and all the Chihuahuas started
racing around in circles. There looked to be too many for
Snatcher and Snooper to catch on their own.

Snatcher looked at a table with a large tablecloth draped across it. "Snooper, you get one end and I will get the other," he said. The two detectives each grabbed hold of an end of the tablecloth. "Now let's run together across the room and get them wrapped up in the cloth," said Snatcher.

Both then ran as fast as they could across the room, gathering up startled chihuahuas in the cloth. When they got to the other end of the room, they tied up the cloth and now had a large bag full of very wriggly and angry Chihuahuas.

"Well done Boss," said Snooper. "There might only be two of us, but we showed them didn't we?"
"Teamwork," said Snatcher.
"That is the secret; working together."

Back at the station Chief Growler was incredibly happy with his two detectives. "Great work, all the bones have been recovered and the bank are very pleased."

Deputy Gruff went into the main office.
"Officer Doodles, please ring the bank and
arrange for the bones to be returned."
"I am Noodles Ma'am, Doodles has a day off today,"
said Noodles.

Deputy Gruff sighed but then thought.
"Name badges, that's the answer!"
She made a note to order some
as soon as possible.

MESSAGE FROM THE CHIEF

Remember children... taking something that doesn't belong to you is wrong. Even if you find it you should hand it to an adult so they can find the owner. The Chihuahua boys will be in the doghouse for a long time.

'Til next time, be good and
keep safe.

ABOUT THE AUTHOR

First time Author Sam Shepherd is a retired
police officer of 32 years service. He is now
a professional Grandad.

WWW.DOGCHESTERPD.COM